NIBI'S WATER SONG

BY **Sunshine Tenasco** ILLUSTRATED BY **Chief Lady Bird**

Lee & Low Books Inc.
New York

Slurrrrp!

Nibi was a thirsty, thirsty girl, so thirsty her mouth was clucking.

Nibi ran to her sink and tried to get water.
Oh no! There was still no clean water.
Hmmm, what should Nibi do?
She ran to her neighbor's house. **NOPE!**
Just brown water there. **Blachhhh!**

No problem. Thirsty, thirsty Nibi skipped down the road to the river.

Kigonz the fish jumped up and told Nibi, "You can't drink this dirty water!"

BLACHHHH! This water was sicky too!

No problem. Nibi skipped to the next town, the town
with the big, shiny houses.

She knocked on the biggest, shiniest door she could
find and said, **"I am thirsty, thirsty Nibi and I need water!**
Do you have water? May I please have some?"

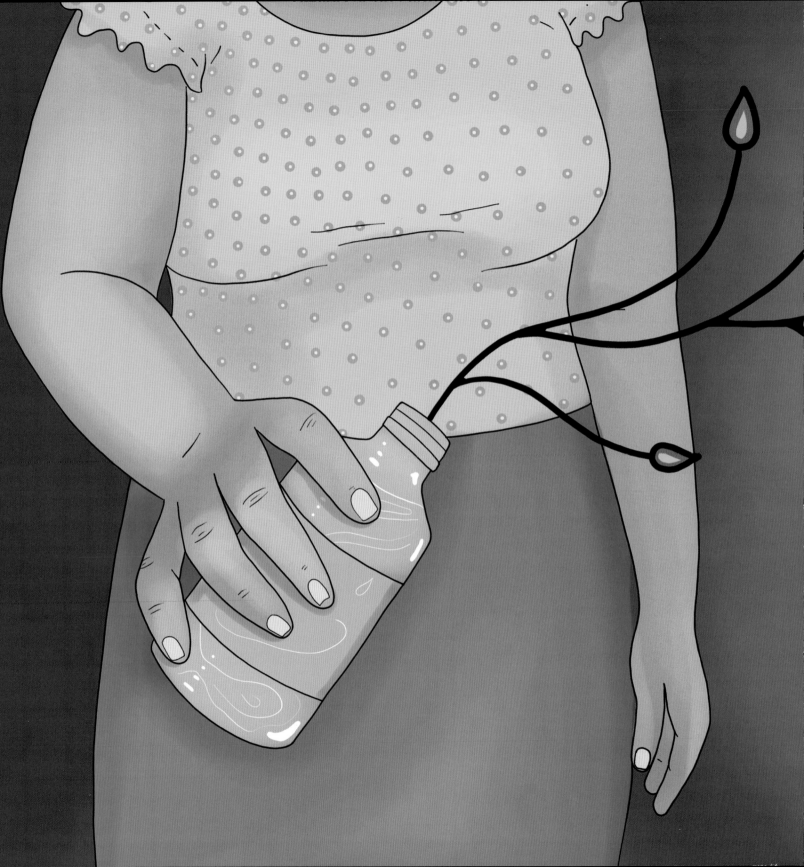

The nice lady who lived in the big house with the shiny door gave her a teeny-tiny plastic bottle of water and shooed her away.

Nibi was so thirsty she drank the bottle of water in one big gulp. **Burp!** Her water was all gone again.

No problem. Thirsty, thirsty Nibi went back to the house with the shiny door and knocked and knocked and knocked . . . and knocked some more. Nobody opened the door this time.

No problem. Thirsty, thirsty Nibi kept knocking on every single door in the town with all the big, shiny houses.

KNOCK, KNOCK, KNOCK, KNOCK, KNOCK, KNOCK!
But no one came out.

Nibi made a sign. She danced and sang down every street with her giant sign.

"I am thirsty, thirsty Nibi and I need water!"

Nibi looked under rocks.
Nibi looked in swamps.
Nibi looked in houses.
Nibi asked all of her friends.
They had no water to share with her either.

But then all of Nibi's friends started singing and dancing with her: **"She is thirsty, thirsty Nibi and she needs water!"**

They were so loud that the people in the big, shiny houses came out. They listened.

And soon they were all singing to Nibi's tune: **"She is thirsty, thirsty Nibi and she needs water."**

The more everyone sang together, the louder they got.
The whole town with the big, shiny houses started
to sing,

"She is thirsty, thirsty Nibi
and we want to
help her have water!"

Nibi gathered all of her new and old friends into one big sharing circle. One by one they voiced their best ideas. Everyone listened. They came up with a way to get Nibi and all of her friends clean water!

Together they danced their way
to the shiniest building, and showed
all the rule-makers how to heal the
water. The rule-makers listened and
stopped making the water sicky.

Soon the water wasn't sicky and everyone could drink it! Thanks to all their hard work, finally thirsty, thirsty Nibi got her clean water, and she shared it with all her friends.

And she was happy, happy Nibi.

Author's Note

I'm from Kitigan Zibi Anishinabeg, a reservation about eighty miles from Ottawa, Ontario, the capital city of Canada. Kitigan Zibi is right beside the French-speaking town of Maniwaki, Quebec. Everyone in Maniwaki has access to clean water, but forty percent of my community can't access this basic human right.

Kitigan Zibi is one of many First Nations communities dealing with this complex issue. The reasons the water is not potable are unique to each place, ranging from agricultural waste and industrial pollution to natural radiation and lack of infrastructure. The water in some communities is drinkable when boiled, but other communities require bottled water to be delivered to their homes.

I started a project called Her Braids to educate Canadians about the water conditions too many First Nations communities face. My original idea was to create tiny pendants with Anishinabe beadwork as conversation starters. The project grew, and now we deliver workshops where people learn how to make their own beaded pendants. We talk about systemic racism and how we can each do our part by raising awareness of this crisis. I am forever grateful to have *Nibi's Water Song* published so that we can all do this important work together.

–Sunshine Tenasco

Illustrator's Note

Working on this project was an important undertaking for me to help educate young people about the ongoing injustices in Indigenous communities across Canada. As of January 2021, there are currently fifty-seven long-term water advisories in thirty-nine communities. One of these communities has had to boil its drinking water since 1995. This is unacceptable, but there are a lot of people fighting for clean water. As an artist, I feel it is important to create work that highlights the beauty and spirit of my community members, many of whom are working hard to advocate for access to clean water. Nibi is wearing a Her Braids pendant, and I use Woodland-style fish and florals to show the love and respect we have for the interconnectedness of all things. When we fight for clean water, we advocate for our health, as well as the health of the land and the animals too. There is a lot at stake and I hope that this book can help inspire change.

–Chief Lady Bird

For my children, Kegona, Nibi, Kiniw and Challa. May you all create your own life with happiness.

For my mom, Luce, who always ordered me Scholastic books, and for teaching so many children to love reading.

And for Pauline Decontie, the teacher who taught more than she ever knew, and for making me write my first book.

—S.T.

For my family and my kin. Mom, Dad, Douglas, Chantel: you help me see the magic in myself.

For Ludo and Cruz: you teach and inspire me to be soft and playful. Miigwech.

—C.L.B.

LEE & LOW BOOKS Inc., 95 Madison Avenue, New York, NY 10016 • leeandlow.com
Edited by Anne Shone (Canada) and Cheryl Klein (US) • US book design by Abby Dening • Book production
by The Kids at Our House • The text is set in Quando, with the display type in Butterfly Ball and the signs in
Patrick Hand. • The illustrations were created digitally. • Manufactured in China by RR Donnelley
10 9 8 7 6 5 4 3 2 1
First Lee & Low Edition

Library of Congress Cataloging-in-Publication Data
Names: Tenasco, Sunshine, author. | Lady Bird, Chief, illustrator.
Title: Nibi's water song / Sunshine Tenasco ; illustrated by Chief Lady Bird.
Description: First edition. | New York : Lee & Low Books, Inc., [2021] | Audience: Ages 3-7. | Audience: Grades
2-3. | Summary: "Nibi, a Native American girl, cannot get clean water from her tap or the river, so she goes on
a journey to connect with fellow water protectors and get clean water for all" -- Provided by publisher.
Identifiers: LCCN 2021010275 | ISBN 9781643794822 (hardcover) | ISBN 9781643794839 (epub)
Subjects: CYAC: Water quality management--Fiction. | Indians of North America--Fiction.
Classification: LCC PZ7.1.T4445 Ni 2021 | DDC [E]--dc23
LC record available at https://lccn.loc.gov/2021010275

MIX
Paper from
responsible sources
FSC® C144853
FSC
www.fsc.org

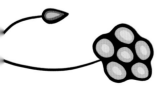